OPEN WIDE!

A Visit to the Dentist

by Cecile Schoberle
illustrated by Barry Goldberg

Simon Spotlight/Nickelodeon

New York   London   Toronto   Sydney   Singapore

Note to Parents

A visit to the dentist's office should be a pleasant and positive experience. Regular checkups will give your children a chance to feel more and more at ease with the dentist and hygienist. In between dental visits remember to stress the importance of brushing and flossing after meals as well as good eating habits to prevent cavities and maintain healthy teeth and gums. Remind your children that the more they brush and floss, the more they'll want to smile and show off their teeth!

KLASKY CSUPOINC.

Based on the TV series *Rugrats*® created by Arlene Klasky, Gabor Csupo, and Paul Germain as seen on Nickelodeon®

SIMON SPOTLIGHT
An imprint of Simon & Schuster Children's Publishing Division
1230 Avenue of the Americas
New York, New York 10020

6 8 10 9 7

ISBN 0-689-82570-6

"Hey, you babies! Guess who I get to go see?" said Angelica.

"Who, Angelica?" asked Chuckie.

The babies were playing in Tommy's front yard. Angelica's dad, Drew, had brought her over to visit.

"I get to go see the dentist," said Angelica. "Just like a growed-up does. You babies are too young to go."

"Why do you get to go see Dennis?" asked Lil.

"Who's Dennis?" asked Phil.

"My daddy said the dentist looks at your teeth," said Angelica.

"We're both going," said Susie. "'Because we've got all of our teeth already."

"Yeah, but you babies don't," said Angelica. She flashed a big, mean smile.

"So why does Dennis look at toofies?" asked Tommy.

"To count 'em," said Angelica.

Tommy tried to get a closer look inside Angelica's mouth. "How many do you have?" he asked.

"Um, about a hunnert billion," Angelica said.

"Hey, I gotta idea!" exclaimed Tommy. "Let's count everybody's toofies."

"Yeah!" shouted Phil. "Me first!"

"No, me first, Philip!" yelled Lil.

Tommy looked in Chuckie's mouth. "One . . . two . . . tree . . . eighty . . . hmm, what number comes next?" he said.

"This is so dumb!" sighed Angelica.

"Teeth help you eat your lunch," said Susie. She crunched on an apple.

"It looks like Chuckie ate spinach," said Tommy.

Tommy's dog, Spike, trotted by as he carried a bone.

"Gee, Spike's toofies look sharp," said Phil.

"I'll bet Reptar's are super sharp!" said Tommy.

"Do you guys remember that TV show about beavers?" asked Lil.

"Yeah, beavers got big toofies. They chewed up a whole tree," said Phil.

"How come?" asked Chuckie.

"Uh, I think they like to make toofpicks," said Phil.

"You know what? Some toofies swim," said Tommy.

"What do you mean?" asked Angelica.

"I saw Grampa's toofies swimming in a glass jar all by themselves," said Tommy.

"Well, my daddy told me I'm going to get a present from the dentist," said Angelica. "A *special* toothbrush!"

"A magic one?" asked Phil.

"Or one that talks like that dolly we saw in the store?" asked Lil.

"Maybe it's got jingle bells," said Tommy.

"You dumb babies! I'm going to get a Cynthia toothbrush like I saw on TV, with shiny gold stars all over it!" said Angelica.

Drew came over to Angelica. "We're taking Susie with us to the dentist's office, Angelica. Her daddy will meet us there," he said.

"We'll stop by, too," said Didi. "After you're finished, we'll all go out to lunch at Burger Doodle."

Drew took Angelica and Susie by the hand. "It's time to show Dr. Pearlies what beautiful teeth you have, my dears."

"Hey, didn't Li'l Reddy Hood say something like that in the story my daddy read us?" whispered Chuckie to Tommy.

"Yeah, I hope they don't meet any woofs on the way," said Tommy.

Angelica and Susie arrived at the dentist's office.

"Do we get cookies?" Angelica asked the lady at the desk.

"Oh, no," she said. "You shouldn't eat too many cookies. They're bad for your teeth."

Angelica said to Susie, "Do you think the dentist can tell how many chocolate chip cookies I ate?"

Susie said, "You mean like Santa knows when you've been bad?"

Angelica said, "Yeah, maybe the Tooth Fairy knows too, and she told the dentist!"

The dentist's helper took Susie into one room, while Drew took Angelica into a room across the hall. Susie waved as Angelica's daddy helped her climb into a big chair.

"Hello, Angelica! I'm Dr. Pearlies!" said the dentist. "We're going to have fun today. First I'm going to take a picture of your teeth."

Angelica loved to have her picture taken. "Make sure you get my best side," she said.

"Mr. Pickles, let's go look at the x-rays," said Dr. Pearlies. They stepped into the hall.

Susie called out to Angelica from the other room, "Hey, Angelica! Do you have a squirty water-hose thing in your room too?"

"Yes, and lots of shiny things," replied Angelica. "Hey, look, Cynthia!" she said to her doll. "Are you ready for the dentist?"

Angelica looked at all of Dr. Pearlies' shiny things.

"Cynthia, I wonder what that brushy thing does?" asked Angelica as she pointed. "Oh, Cynthia, are you scared? But Dr. Pearlies seems so nice. Wait, Cynthia! Don't run away!"

The doll flew across the room.

Angelica called, "Oh, no! I'm coming, Cynthia!"

Angelica was upset. "Oh, my poor Cynthia!" she yelled. Angelica grabbed a cup and flipped a little switch that turned on the water faucet. Water gushed to the floor. She raced over to Cynthia and tried to give her a drink.

Drew and Dr. Pearlies came back into the room. Drew held up the x-ray pictures. He said, "Just as I thought. My little princess has perfect . . . AARRGH!"

The place was a mess!

"Princess, what happened?" asked Drew.

Angelica held up her doll. "Look, Daddy! Cynthia's got no cavitrees!"

Out in the waiting room, Didi arrived with the babies to pick up the girls.

"What a cute baby!" the receptionist exclaimed. Dil gurgled.

"What do you think Angelica and Susie are doing right now?" Chuckie asked Tommy.

"Maybe they get to try out wearing new kinds of toofies," said Tommy.

"Yeah, like a beaver!" said Phil.

"Or like Spike!" said Lil.

"Or like Reptar!" said Tommy.

Angelica and Susie went back to the waiting room.
Susie's dad, Randy Carmichael, had just arrived.

"Hello, Susie!" said Randy.

"Hi, Daddy!" Susie exclaimed. "Look at these great
party bags we got!"

"What's inside, dear?" asked Randy.

"Are there any chocolate chip cookies?" asked Angelica.

"No, but there's lots of other cool stuff," said Susie.

"Just gimme my toothbrush with the gold stars!" said Angelica
as she dug through her bag.

"Did you get a Cynthia toothbrush with gold stars on it, Angelica?" asked Tommy.

Angelica couldn't find one. "No, but I got something *much* better!" she said. "I got a great *big* gold star! All for me! 'Cause I did so good at the dentist!"

"Wow!" said Tommy. "I can't wait till I have lots of toofies. Then I can get a big gold star too!"